Ricky Ricotta's Giant Robot vs the Voodoo Vultures from Venus

Ricky Ricotta's Giant Robot vs the Voodoo Vultures from Venus

The Third Robot Adventure Novel by
DAV PILKEY

Pictures by
MARTIN ONTIVEROS

SCHOLASTIC

For Justin Libertowski – D. P.

*To Bwana, Chloe, Trixy and Guy – AND
especially Micki and our little expected
young 'un – we can't wait to meet you!* – M. O.

Scholastic Children's Books,
Commonwealth House, 1-19 New Oxford Street,
London, WC1A 1NU, UK
a division of Scholastic Ltd
London ~ New York ~ Toronto ~ Sydney ~ Auckland
Mexico City ~ New Delhi ~ Hong Kong

First published in the US by Scholastic Inc., 2001

First published in the UK by Scholastic Ltd, 2002

Text copyright © Dav Pilkey, 2001
Illustrations copyright © Martin Ontiveros, 2001

ISBN 0 439 99437 3

Printed and bound in Great Britain by Cox & Wyman Ltd, Reading, Berks

2 4 6 8 10 9 7 5 3 1

Chapters

CHAPTER 1

Late for Supper

It was supper time at the Ricotta home. Ricky's father was sitting at the table. Ricky's mother was sitting at the table. But Ricky was not sitting at the table.

And neither was his giant Robot.

"It is six o'clock," said Ricky's father. "Ricky and his giant Robot are late for supper again."

Just then, Ricky and his giant Robot flew in.

"Sorry we are late," said Ricky.
"We were in Hawaii collecting
seashells."

"You have been late for supper three times this week," said Ricky's mother. "No more TV until you boys learn some responsibility."

"No TV?" cried Ricky. "But *Rocket Rodent* is on tonight. Everybody on Earth will be watching it!"

"Everybody but you two," said Ricky's father.

CHAPTER 2

Responsibility

That night, Ricky and his giant Robot went to bed early. They camped in the back garden under the stars.

"I wish we could watch TV tonight," said Ricky.

Ricky's Robot unscrewed his hand, and out popped a big-screen television.

"No, giant Robot," said Ricky. "We're not allowed. We've got to learn some responsibility first."

Ricky's giant Robot did not
know what "responsibility" was.
"Responsibility," said Ricky,
"is doing the right thing at the
right time."

Ricky and his giant Robot
were pretty good at doing
the right thing . . .

. . . but they had trouble
with the *right time* part.

17

CHAPTER 3

Victor Von Vulture

At that very moment, over forty million kilometres away, there lived an evil vulture on the planet Venus.

Temperature: 480 degrees. . . Only 2,915 hours till sunset. . . Today's forecast: mostly gassy (with a chance of sulphuric acid)

His name was Victor Von Vulture, and he hated living on Venus.

It was so hot on Venus that everyone's food was always ruined. Their toasted cheese sandwiches were always *way too gooey . . .*

. . . they had to drink their
chocolate bars with straws . . .

. . . and everybody's ice cream melted before they could even get one lick!

So Victor Von Vulture
decided to move to Earth
where the eating was good.

First, he gathered an army of the biggest Voodoo Vultures he could find.

Then he invented a voodoo remote control and pointed it at Earth.

"When I press this button,"
said Victor, "an evil voodoo
beam will shoot through space.
And when it reaches Earth, the
planet will be OURS!"

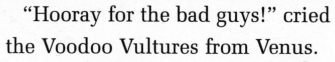

"Hooray for the bad guys!" cried
the Voodoo Vultures from Venus.

CHAPTER 4

Voodoo Rays from Outer Space

Ricky and his giant Robot fell asleep under the stars, while everyone else in town was watching television.

29

Suddenly, a voodoo ray from outer
space beamed down through the
night sky. The strange signal was
picked up by all the TVs in town.

30

The screens began to glow eerily
as a strange voice came from the
wicked signal.

"Obey the Voodoo Vultures!"
said the voice. "Obey the Voodoo
Vultures!"

Soon, every mouse in the city
was hypnotized.

CHAPTER 5

Breakfast with the Robot

The next morning, Ricky woke up and went inside to make breakfast. But all the food in the house was gone.

"Hey!" said Ricky. "Where's all the food? I can't go to school without breakfast!"

Ricky's Robot knew just what
to do. He flew straight to Florida.
A few seconds later, he returned
with an orange tree.

"Thanks, giant Robot," said
Ricky. "I love freshly squeezed
orange juice! Now may I have a
doughnut?"

Ricky's giant Robot flew off
again. Soon he returned with
some fresh doughnuts.

"Hey!" Ricky laughed. "I said *a*
doughnut . . . not a doughnut
shop! Please put that back, and
bring me some milk!"

Ricky's Robot flew away again.
This time he returned with the
freshest milk he could find.

"Ummm. . . " said Ricky. "I
think I'll skip the milk today!"

CHAPTER 6

Obey the Voodoo Vultures

After breakfast, the giant Robot
flew Ricky straight to school.
But something was not right!

All the mice in school had strange looks on their faces.

They were all carrying food out of the cafeteria door, straight to the centre of town.

Ricky found his reading teacher, Miss Swiss.

"What's going on here?" asked Ricky.

"Obey the Voodoo Vultures," said Miss Swiss.

Then Ricky saw his maths teacher,
Mr Mozzarella.

"Aren't we supposed to have a
test today?" asked Ricky.

"Obey the Voodoo Vultures," said
Mr Mozzarella.

Finally, Ricky found Principal
Provolone.

"Where is everybody going
with all this food?" asked Ricky.

"Obey the Voodoo Vultures,"
said Principal Provolone.

Ricky was not getting any
answers.

"Come on, Robot," said Ricky.
"We've got to get to the bottom of
this!"

CHAPTER 7

Those Vicious Vultures

Ricky and his giant Robot followed the long line of mice to the centre of town. There, they saw a horrible sight!

A small army of giant vultures had taken over the city and turned everybody into voodoo slaves. The hungry vultures were eating every bite of food in town.

"We want more chocolate chip cookies!" yelled one of the vultures.

"Yesss, masters," said the mice as they scurried off to start baking.

"And no more *rice cakes*!" yelled another vulture.

47

"We've got to stop those evil vultures," Ricky whispered. "But how?"

Ricky and his giant Robot looked around. They saw Victor and his evil invention.

"I'll bet those vultures are controlling everybody with that remote control," said Ricky. "We've got to get it away from them." But that was going to be tricky.

The remote control was right in the centre of town where all the vultures could keep an eye on it.

"Hmmm," said Ricky. "What we need is a *distraction*."

CHAPTER 8

Ricky's Recipe

Ricky and his giant Robot hurried back to school. In the cafeteria kitchen, Ricky mixed some flour and milk in a large bowl. Then he added sugar, eggs and chocolate chips.

"Now comes the secret ingredient," said Ricky.

The giant Robot flew straight to
Mexico and returned with the
hottest chillies he could find.

Ricky stirred the cookie batter while his giant Robot added hundreds of SUPER RED-HOT CHILLI PEPPERS to the mix.

The giant Robot quickly baked
the cookies with his microwave
eyeballs, then cooled the pan
with his super-freezy breath.

CHAPTER 9

Dinner Is Served

Ricky and his giant Robot returned to the centre of town. Ricky pretended he was hypnotized as he bravely carried his cookies towards the Voodoo Vultures.

"It's about time!" said one of the
vultures.

"Gimme those cookies!" said
another.

The greedy vultures were fighting
over Ricky's cookies. They stuffed
them into their mouths as
fast as they could.

Suddenly, the vultures' eyes got
very big. Their faces turned bright
red and steam came out of their ears.

"OUCHIE! OUCHIE! *OUCHIE!*"
screamed the vultures as they danced
around in pain.

The vultures were distracted, so Ricky's giant Robot reached for the remote control.

He grabbed the evil invention in his mighty fist and crushed it with one powerful squeeze.

Suddenly, all the mice in town returned to normal. They screamed at the sight of the Voodoo Vultures, and everybody ran straight home. Ricky's giant Robot had saved the city . . . but Victor Von Vulture had other plans.

CHAPTER 10

Ricky's Bright Idea

Victor Von Vulture grabbed Ricky
with his claw. "Don't come any
closer, giant Robot," said Victor, "or
I will destroy your little friend!"

The Voodoo Vultures were very angry. They huffed and they puffed as they surrounded Ricky's giant Robot.

"You're going to be sorry you tricked us!" said Victor Von Vulture, as he flew higher and higher.

Just when everything seemed
hopeless, Ricky had an idea.

He reached up and grabbed a feather from Victor Von Vulture's rear end. Ricky yanked the feather out.

"*Ouch!*" yelled Victor.

Ricky wiggled the feather under Victor's claw.

"H-hey! S-s-stop that! It tickles!"
laughed Victor Von Vulture.

But Ricky did not stop. He wiggled
the feather faster and faster. Victor
began laughing harder and harder.

Finally, Victor Von Vulture
let go of Ricky. The little mouse
fell through the air. . .

CHAPTER 11

Robo-Rescue

Ricky was in big trouble. He was falling through the sky, faster and faster.

"Help me, giant Robot!" Ricky cried.

With lightning speed, the giant Robot's arm shot up into the air. The giant Robot caught Ricky by the back of his T-shirt . . .

. . . and set him down safely in a tree. "Thanks, buddy," said Ricky. "Now go get 'em!"

CHAPTER 12

The Battle Begins

The giant Robot flew up and grabbed Victor in his mighty fist.

"Help, Voodoo Vultures, HELP!!!" yelled Victor.

Suddenly, the evil Voodoo
Vultures got ready to attack. The
giant Robot was outnumbered.

"This is going to be fun,"
Victor snarled.

The Voodoo Vultures began
to attack.

The giant Robot defended
himself.

"Hey, wait a minute, Robot,"
said Victor. "Put me down first!"
But the giant Robot did not have
time to put Victor down. Victor was
stuck in the middle of the fight.

Every time the giant Robot punched, Victor felt the blow!

Every time the giant Robot clobbered, Victor got clobbered, too!

Every time the giant Robot clunked heads, Victor got the worst of it!

"Ouchie, ouchie, *ouchie!*" cried Victor Von Vulture. "This is not as much fun as I thought it would be!"

CHAPTER 13

The Big Battle

(IN FLIP-O-RAMA™)

O.RAMA

HERE'S HOW IT WORKS!

STEP 1
Place your *left* hand inside the dotted lines marked "LEFT HAND HERE". Hold the book open *flat*.

STEP 2
Grasp the *right-hand* page with your right thumb and index finger (inside the dotted lines marked "RIGHT THUMB HERE").

STEP 3
Now *quickly* flip the right-hand page back and forth until the picture appears to be *animated*.

(For extra fun, try adding your own sound effects!)

FLIP-O-RAMA 1

(pages 87 and 89)

Remember, flip *only* page 87.
While you are flipping, make sure
you can see the picture on page 87
and the one on page 89.
If you flip quickly, the two
pictures will start to look like
<u>one</u> *animated* picture.

Don't forget to add
your own sound effects!

LEFT HAND HERE

The Voodoo Vultures
Attacked.

RIGHT
THUMB
HERE

The Voodoo Vultures
Attacked.

FLIP-O-RAMA 2

(pages 91 and 93)

Remember, flip *only* page 91.
While you are flipping, make sure
you can see the picture on page 91
and the one on page 93.
If you flip quickly, the two
pictures will start to look like
<u>one</u> *animated* picture.

Don't forget to add
your own sound effects!

LEFT HAND HERE

Ricky's Robot
Fought Back.

Ricky's Robot
Fought Back.

FLIP-O-RAMA 3

(pages 95 and 97)

Remember, flip *only* page 95.
While you are flipping, make sure
you can see the picture on page 95
and the one on page 97.
If you flip quickly, the two
pictures will start to look like
<u>one</u> *animated* picture.

Don't forget to add
your own sound effects!

LEFT HAND HERE

The Voodoo Vultures
Battled Hard.

The Voodoo Vultures
Battled Hard.

FLIP-O-RAMA 4

(pages 99 and 101)

Remember, flip *only* page 99.
While you are flipping, make sure
you can see the picture on page 99
and the one on page 101.
If you flip quickly, the two
pictures will start to look like
<u>one</u> *animated* picture.

Don't forget to add
your own sound effects!

LEFT HAND HERE

Ricky's Robot
Battled Harder.

99

RIGHT THUMB HERE

Ricky's Robot Battled Harder.

FLIP-O-RAMA 5

(pages 103 and 105)

Remember, flip *only* page 103.
While you are flipping, make sure
you can see the picture on page 103
and the one on page 105.
If you flip quickly, the two
pictures will start to look like
<u>one</u> *animated* picture.

Don't forget to add
your own sound effects!

LEFT HAND HERE

Ricky's Robot
Saved the Day!

RIGHT
THUMB
HERE

Ricky's Robot
Saved the Day!

CHAPTER 14

Justice Prevails

The evil Voodoo Vultures were no match for Ricky Ricotta's giant Robot. "Let's get out of here!" moaned the vultures.

"Hey, wait for *ME*!" cried Victor Von Vulture. But it was too late. The Voodoo Vultures flew back to Venus and were never heard from again.

107

The giant Robot picked up Ricky, and together they took Victor Von Vulture to the Squeakyville Prison.

"Boo-hoo-hoo!" cried Victor.

"Maybe now you will learn some responsibility!" said Ricky.

Then Ricky Ricotta and his
giant Robot flew straight home . . .

. . . just in time for supper.

CHAPTER 15

Supper Time

Ricky's mother and father had cooked a wonderful feast for Ricky and his giant Robot.

"Oh boy!" said Ricky. "TV dinners! My favourite!"

"We're both very proud of you boys," said Ricky's mother.

"Thank you for doing the right thing at the right time," said Ricky's father.

"No problem," said Ricky . . .

"that's what friends are for."

HOW TO DRAW RICKY

1.

2.

3.

4.

5.

6.

1.

2.

3.

4.

5.

6.

HOW TO DRAW RICKY'S ROBOT

1.

2.

3.

4.

5.

6.

HOW TO DRAW
VICTOR VON VULTURE

1.

2.

3.

4.

5.

6.

1.

2.

3.

4.

5.

6.

HOW TO DRAW
A VOODOO VULTURE

1.

2.

3.

4.

5.

6.

1.

2.

3.

4.

5.

6.

125

COMING SOON:

Ricky Ricotta's Giant Robot

vs

The Mecha-Monkeys from Mars

The Jurassic Jack Rabbits from Jupiter

The Stupid Stinkbugs from Saturn

The Uranium Unicorns from Uranus

The Naughty Night Crawlers from Neptune

The Un-Pleasant Penguins from Pluto

About the Author and Illustrator

DAV PILKEY created his first stories as comic books while he was in elementary school. In 1997, he wrote and illustrated his first adventure novel for children, *The Adventures of Captain Underpants*, which received rave reviews and was an instant best-seller — as were the other books that followed in the series. Dav is also the creator of numerous award-winning picture books. He and his dog live in Seattle, Washington.

It was a stroke of luck when Dav discovered the work of artist **MARTIN ONTIVEROS**. Dav knew that Martin was just the right illustrator for the Ricky Ricotta's Giant Robot series. Martin lives in Portland, Oregon. He has a lot of toys as well as two cats, Bunny and Spanky.

Visit Dav Pilkey's Extra-Crunchy
Web Site O'Fun at:
www.pilkey.com